Christmas by the Lake

Christmas by the Lake

Drew Beyson

Inner Council Publications

Christmas by the Lake

Copyright © **2024** Drew Beyson

All rights reserved.

No part of this publication may be reproduced, distributed, or transmitted in any form or by any means, including photocopying, recording, or other electronic or mechanical methods, without the prior written permission of the publisher, except as permitted by U.S. copyright law. For permission requests, contact info@innercouncilpublications.com.

The story, all names, characters, and incidents portrayed in this production are fictitious. No identification with actual persons (living or deceased), places, buildings, and products is intended or should be inferred.

ISBN: 979-8-9939767-1-6 (paperback)

Paperback edition published 2025.

Contents

It's Time

7 Days before Christmas

JULIE STOOD BY THE window of her lakeside cabin, watching the snow fall outside. The wind rattled the panes, but inside, the world was still. It had been five long years since Ted's unexpected death—spent numbly going through the motions of life, each of the past few Christmases feeling heavier than the last.

She sighed, her breath fogging up the glass. *Has it really been that long?*

This lake had always been her refuge, a place where she escaped the noise of the world. For the past four holiday seasons, she hadn't even bothered to decorate. She felt repelled when she got close to the closet where the decorations were placed. The thought of hanging garlands, trimming a tree, or celebrating the season without Ted had been unbearable. Yet today, something felt different. A gentle stir in the air, a lightness she hadn't felt in years. Maybe it was time to stop carrying her grief like a burden. Maybe **this** Christmas, she could finally let herself feel the joy of the season again.

Her eyes drifted to the closet where she'd stored her Christmas decorations, untouched for years. *Is it really time?* Her heart tightened at the thought. She didn't know if she was ready. After a few hesitations to get those decorations, a quiet voice whispered inside it was okay. *It's time.*

Across the snow-covered yard, the Riley children played, their bright and carefree laughter ringing out. Their parents, Bill and Joan, tugged the children along on sleds, their faces rosy from the cold. Watching them stirred Julie to recall how she couldn't have children, but she quickly overcame that feeling with the enjoyment of seeing them play together.

Her smile held a hint of both happiness and sadness, a reminder of the joyful holidays she and Ted had spent in this very place before everything changed. Now, the sight of the children didn't bring tears to her eyes. Instead, it sparked a longing—a wish for a new beginning.

Without allowing herself to second-guess, Julie went to the closet and opened the door. She found the boxes of Christmas decorations tucked away in the back, still packed exactly the way she had left them all those years ago. She hesitated, her fingers hovering over the lid. The memories of brighter Christmases' past overcame her thoughts. Slowly, she pulled the boxes out and carried them to the living room.

As she unpacked the tangle of lights and ornaments, vivid Christmas memories played in her mind, not with the familiar sting of grief but with a warm feeling. She recalled how Ted had his battles with the lights and why they were in a tangle when she found them. The artificial tree that had always been the center of their holidays was waiting in its box, ready to bring color and life back into her cabin. As Julie set it up, she felt the release of the past lift with each action she took.

I haven't smiled a real, genuine smile in years. I'm ready, she thought. *I'm ready for this.*

The sharp ring of her phone pulled her out of her thoughts. It was her sister, Eleanor.

"Hey, Julie!" Eleanor's voice was bright, filled with the sounds of children's laughter in the background. "Just wanted to check in. Did you make it to the cabin, okay? The kids are driving me crazy with excitement about Christmas—it's been non-stop chaos around here."

"I'm here," Julie said, her voice lighter than usual. "Got in yesterday. I stocked the fridge with what I brought, but I still need to pick up a few things from the store. And... believe it or not, I'm decorating for Christmas."

There was a pause at the other end of the line. "Really?" Eleanor's voice softened with surprise. "That's wonderful, Julie. I'm so happy to hear you say that. It's been too long."

"I think it's time," Julie said, looking at the half-assembled tree. "I'm ready to enjoy the holidays again. I might even bake some Christmas sugar cookies later."

"I'm glad to hear it," Eleanor replied warmly. "Just take it easy, okay? The roads are getting bad with all the snow. Stay safe and warm up there."

"I will," Julie promised, smiling at her sister's concern. "Give the kids my love."

After hanging up, Julie finished assembling the tree, wrapping the lights all around the tree. When she put the plug into the outlet, the light bulbs lit up the room with a cheery glow.

She remembered she needed to get to the supermarket and unplugged the lights. Finding her car fob on the kitchen table, she bundled up in her coat and gloves and prepared to head into town. The snowfall continued. The wind bit at her cheeks, but she didn't notice and focused instead on the excitement of filling her cart with holiday essentials.

When she arrived, the supermarket was busy, filled with holiday shoppers.

Julie grabbed an available cart and maneuvered through the crowded aisles, picking up the essentials: flour, sugar, eggs, and a few festive cookie cutters. As she stood in the baking aisle, her eyes fell on a jar of cinnamon.

She paused as memories of Ted surged back. He had loved cinnamon in his coffee, always insisting that no holiday was complete without its warm, comforting scent filling the air.

Her fingers brushed the jar, and for a moment, the familiar pang of grief surfaced—sharp, quick, and almost reflexive. But this time, the pain didn't linger. It faded just as fast, leaving behind only a gentle ache, a reminder that his memory felt more warm than sorrowful. With a small smile, she placed the cinnamon in her cart.

This year, I'm bringing cinnamon home.

Julie moved through the store, her cart now filled with eggs, pancake mix, whipped cream, cocoa, sprinkles, and even a small standing rib roast for Christmas dinner. She grabbed a couple of frozen pizzas and other foods, and she found a nice loaf of sourdough bread. By the time she reached the checkout, her mood had lightened, a subtle but welcome shift. The young cashier, Tina, smiled brightly as she scanned the items.

"Looks like you're planning a fun Christmas," Tina said.

Julie's face lit up with a smile, and her heart lifted with a newfound sense of joy. "Yeah, I believe that I am."

After loading the bags into her trunk, she headed back to the cabin and enjoyed the beauty of another sunset, as the days were growing shorter now.

On her drive home, the pink and purple hues reflected off the snow-covered lake when she pulled up to her cabin. As she unloaded her groceries, the colors became more intense and enjoyable as the sun sank for the night. Once inside, she lit a fire in the fireplace, the crackling warmth filling the room. But she didn't sense the warmth as she focused on the decorations and plugged in the tree lights. She took a moment to breathe in the cozy atmosphere, seeing the twinkling tree in the corner. The smell of pine and wood smoke from the logs filled her home.

The kettle whistled, and Julie prepared a cup of Earl Grey tea. She carried the cup to her chair in the living room and sat down to enjoy it. Julie looked at the decorations she had unpacked, feeling contentment she hadn't felt in years. Tomorrow, she would finish decorating the tree. Tonight, she will simply enjoy this newfound peace and the bright lights from the tree.

Just as she began to unwind, a knock on the door startled her.

Julie stood up, staring at the door, surprised by the knock. The quiet cabin, so wrapped in solitude and warmth, seemed to hold its breath as she stared at the door.

Who could be coming to see me?

She went to the door, turning the porch light on, looked through the peephole, and opened the door.

The Unexpected Guest

7 Days before Christmas

WHEN JULIE OPENED THE door, a man stood on her porch, his hair dusted with snowflakes and his expression calm yet tired.

"Hi," he said, showing a polite smile. "I'm Robert Greyson, staying next door. My cabin's electricity is out, and I was hoping you could help. I have a flashlight."

Julie wasn't prepared for anyone to show up or to deal with a problem. She was expecting solitude this holiday season, but now a man was standing at her door.

"Oh," she said, shaking herself out of her stupor. "Hi. I'm Julie Timmens. Sure, I can help you."

They walked over to Robert's cabin as Robert turned on his flashlight. As they entered the cabin, Julie went to the circuit breaker box, knowing where it was. She saw the main switch was turned off. Once she pushed up the switch, the electricity flowed. They both looked around, and everything seemed to be working. The lights came on, the heat was turned on, and warm air started pushing through the vents.

"Thanks very much for your help, Julie. When I came here in the past, the electricity was on!""Glad I could help you, Robert. The circuit boxes, as you can see, aren't easy to find."

"Sorry to bother you. Now I know where it is!" he said, shoving his hands into his pockets. "I saw the lights on and thought I'd introduce myself and see if you could help me with the power. My cabin isn't looking as cheery as yours through your window. You have done a wonderful job with the decorations!"

"Thank you, no bother. Glad to help. How about coming over to my cabin for a bit? It's freezing in here. Let the heat warm up your cabin. There are logs out back under the tarp when you want to get a fire going. I just started decorating." *It's been so long since I invited anyone in. Should I have done that? Perhaps it wouldn't be so bad to have a bit of company this Christmas.*

"Thanks... I'd like to come over and get warm. I appreciate your kindness."

Inside Julie's cabin, they both enjoyed the warmth from the crackling fire, casting a warm glow across the room. Robert rubbed his hands together, his cheeks still pink from the cold. Julie motioned for him to take a seat by the fireplace, and he thanked her.

"Would you like some Earl Grey tea?"

As she set another mug on the table, Julie took a moment to study him. He looked tired but not worn down, certain it was from having traveled a long way and slowing down.

"Sure, that would be great, thank you."

After adding more water to the kettle, she set it on the stove. It whistled soon after.

"It's good to have a neighbor this Christmas," she said, pouring the tea. The smell of the Earl Grey filled the room as she gave Robert the mug. "I didn't realize your cabin had been rented out."

"Yeah, I just got here. I've been coming here for years, usually in the Spring. It's nice to have a change of pace."

"I've been coming to this cabin for many years. Usually... well, lately alone." The words hung in the air a little too long, and Julie regretted the awkwardness they carried.

"It's a great place for solitude, isn't it?"

She nodded, but in her mind, the idea of solitude felt different now that Robert was sitting across from her. It wasn't unwelcome, though. There was something comforting about not being entirely alone this year.

After a few sips of tea, the conversation turned to more neutral ground—they both shared their favorite local spots and stories of visits to the lake.

Julie mentioned more snow was expected this year than last. They found an easy rhythm, exchanging brief tales of past winters.

"I love the way a lake looks when it's frozen," his voice soft as he glanced out the window, seeing only darkness.

Julie felt a tug of understanding. "That's part of why I come here. The stillness and quiet this time of year... it's different from anywhere else I have been."

There was a moment of quiet, the kind that didn't feel heavy but comfortable, as if they were both content to share each other's company.

"So, are you here for Christmas or through winter?" Robert asked, his tone casual but curious.

Julie hesitated. "I am here for Christmas, then heading back to work at my gallery." The word *Christmas* felt joyful now, unlike the past four years. "I haven't celebrated in a long time, but this year feels different, and I am enjoying the Christmas spirit."

"Same here. I haven't done Christmas since..." He trailed off, and Julie sensed a burden in his unsaid words.

A shared understanding passed between them. It wasn't necessary to explain everything at that moment. They each carried their own history, and they each knew about living with loss.

"I was just about to bake some cookies," Julie said, hoping to lighten the mood. "For the Riley kids next door. I haven't baked them cookies in years. Let's have some fun!"

Robert's face brightened. "Cookies? I haven't had homemade cookies in a while," he added with a playful grin. "I've never been one to turn down dessert."

Julie laughed. "Well, you're welcome to help. I could use a hand." It had been a long time since she'd laughed like this.

"I'd be happy to," Robert said, standing up from his chair. "Just tell me what to do."

Together, they moved into the kitchen.

Julie handed Robert a mixing bowl, and soon, they were measuring ingredients and mixing dough. As they worked, the cabin filled with the warm, familiar scent of cinnamon, the holiday felt real to Julie again.

Once the cookies were in the oven, they settled back by the fire, enjoying their mugs of tea.

"I didn't expect company," Julie admitted, her gaze lingering on the flickering flames. "But I think it's a pleasant surprise."

Robert chuckled. "Neither did I. It's nice. Sometimes, the best moments are the ones we don't plan."

Julie began feeling a warmth in her chest. She planned to spend the holidays alone, wrapped in memories and solitude. But perhaps this was better, sharing the moment with someone who understood and appreciated the value of quiet and reflection.

They sat in comfortable silence from time to time. The aroma of baking cookies filled the room, bringing smiles to their faces as the timer chimed. Julie took the cookies out of the oven and let them cool.

"Would you like to try a cookie, Robert?"

"Absolutely. Could I get one with the colorful sprinkles?"

"Sure. You sounded like a kid just then." Julie laughed.

"These are tasty sugar cookies, and I love the designs, too. I like the cardamom; I don't think I've ever had it before. Thanks, Julie. These cookies remind me of Christmases from long ago. I am sure the Riley kids are going to enjoy them tomorrow!"

Robert glanced at his watch. "I should head back before it gets too late. Thanks for letting me spend time with you this evening."

"I'm glad you came over; I enjoyed your company tonight."

As they walked to the door, Robert hesitated. "Thanks again for helping me with the electricity. Maybe we can meet again? I'd love to hear more about your time at this lake."

Julie smiled, feeling a spark of something new. "You are welcome. I'd like that."

With a final nod, Robert stepped out into the snow, the cold air rushing in as the door opened. "Have a good night, Julie."

"Good night, Robert," feeling his words settle warmly in her chest.

She watched him disappear into the dark and couldn't shake the feeling that something had shifted. As she looked at the fire, Julie felt the warmth of a new beginning settling within her, filling the cabin with feelings she thought she'd lost.

A stirring inside her brought a new energy of hope, a new beginning!

Growing Connection

6 Days before Christmas

AFTER HAVING BREAKFAST, HE got his carvings out on the table in his cabin. Robert set out for Julie's cabin, appreciating the fresh layer of snow that covered the lake and cabins. Each step felt lighter than in recent years. The challenges of work stress he brought to the cabin from the past months seemed to dissolve in the tranquility of being at the lake. He enjoyed the untouched blanket of snow that had fallen overnight, covering the entire area around the cabins and the frozen lake. The thick clouds overhead reflected the twinkling Christmas lights from the cabins, casting a faint, warm hue over the peaceful scene.

As Robert approached Julie's cabin, the decorations on her porch greeted him with a welcoming embrace. Twinkling lights, a festive wreath on the door, and the subtle scent of pine and wood smoke in the air called back pleasant memories.

It was a stark contrast to the cold, barren landscape of the lake and the simplicity of his undecorated cabin. Yet, he found Julie's cabin comforting rather than overwhelming.

Moments after he knocked on the door, Julie appeared with a bright smile. "Come on in! I just pulled two trays of sugar cookies out of the oven," she said, letting Robert in from the cold.

The smell of the cookies and the warmth from the fireplace greeted Robert like old friends as he entered, wrapping him in the familiar, comforting atmosphere. He hadn't realized how much he missed this—the smell of fresh-baked cookies, the flickering glow of a fire, and the simple, heartwarming presence of another person. Shedding his coat, he felt the tension he carried melt away.

Robert glanced around the room, taking in the festive decorations that filled the space. Garlands draped the windows, ornaments sparkled on the tree, and stockings hung neatly by the fire. The cozy holiday cheer that Julie allowed into her home tugged at his heart in ways he hadn't expected. He thought about how he hadn't allowed himself to feel this kind of warmth in years.

As Robert sat at the kitchen table, Julie slid a plate of freshly baked sugar cookies toward him. Robert took a bite of the cookie, savoring the sweetness and warmth. "These are still incredible," he said, smiling at her. "I am enjoying these cookies so much, Julie."

Julie laughed, her eyes twinkling in the firelight. "Thank you. It's one of the few traditions I've kept. My secret ingredient is cardamom, and my husband Ted's was cinnamon. He loved baking with me, especially at Christmas. After he passed, it felt comforting to make these cookies with our secret ingredients."

Robert nodded, "I'm sorry about Ted." Appreciating the power of her tradition, his gaze drifted once again to the decorations, each item telling its own story of holiday memories.

"You've created something special here," he remarked, a note of admiration in his voice. "I haven't decorated for years, but seeing this... it makes me think maybe I should."

"Thank you, Robert." Julie's expression softened, her voice quieter. "I wasn't sure I would decorate this year either. But something about this Christmas... it felt like it was time. Time to let the heaviness go." It had been years since she'd spoken about Ted without sadness overwhelming her, but with Robert, talking about him felt unexpectedly... comforting.

Robert felt relief in her words. It was a sentiment he could relate to. The conversation became more reflective. Losing her husband was palpable, yet in their exchanges, he saw a new hope in her—a desire to move forward.

Julie's eyes shifted to the fire. "It took me years to even consider celebrating Christmas again. After Ted passed, it felt like everything just... stopped. I didn't know how to enjoy the holidays without him. But this year, the energy feels different. I think I've been holding on to that grief for too long."

Robert sat listening, his chest tightening with the familiarity of her words. "I understand. My daughter, Lexi, was the same way with Christmas. She loved sculpting, especially around the holidays. Every year, she'd make ornaments—little snowmen, reindeer, Santas. After she died, I couldn't even look at those things. It took me months to pick up sculpting without her, but when I finally did, it was like... like I found a way to keep her close." As he spoke about Lexi, Robert felt a weight lifting, realizing he hadn't shared these memories with anyone before. He hadn't realized how much he needed to talk about her until now.

Julie's expression grew tender, reaching across the table, touching his arm. "I'm so sorry about Lexi, Robert. I can't imagine how difficult that must have been."

"Thank you. Sculpting became more than a hobby after Lexi passed—it became my way of healing. It's how I stay connected to her. It's been two years," he said.

Julie nodded, her hand still resting on his arm. "I am glad she gave you sculpting... that's what art does for us—it helps us heal. Painting became my lifeline after Ted died. It was the one thing that made me feel like I could still create something beautiful, even in the midst of all that pain."

The warmth between them grew in the moments that followed, the crackling fire the only sound in the room. There was no need to fill the silence with words—each of them understood the other's grief without explanation. And yet, in that shared space of loss, there was renewal, as if by sharing their stories, they were helping each other heal.

After a few moments, Robert shifted the conversation, steering it toward something lighter. "You mentioned earlier that you paint," he said, genuine curiosity in his voice. "What kind of painting do you do?"

Julie smiled, her face lighting up as she spoke about her passion. "I use acrylic or oil paints and paint landscapes—lakes, mountains, sometimes even the desert. And sometimes portraits now and then. I run an art gallery where I sell my work, along with pieces from other artists in the area. We even sell online now."

"That's impressive," Robert said, his interest piqued. "I've never thought about selling my sculptures. They've always been personal, something I do for myself."

Julie raised an eyebrow, smiling. "You should consider it. I'd love to see your work, and maybe we could even showcase them at the art gallery. You might be surprised at how many people would connect with it."

Robert chuckled, shaking his head. "I'm not sure my work is good enough for that, but... I'll think about it."

Julie understood his hesitancy. "Art isn't about being perfect. It's about connection. If your work has meaning to you, it will resonate with others. Art always finds its way to the people who need it most."

Her words lingered in his mind, and Robert found himself considering the possibility. Maybe sharing his sculptures could be another way to honor Lexi's memory by allowing others to see and feel the connection he had with her through his work.

Their conversation continued, touching on topics including art, holiday traditions, and the peacefulness of the lake. Julie marveled at how natural it felt to talk with Robert, how comfortable she was in his presence. It had been a long time since she felt this kind of ease with someone.

Robert wasn't expecting to enjoy Julie's company as much as he did. There was something about her—something that made him feel better, as his grief lessened when he was around her.

Their time today drew to a close. Robert stood, stretching before reaching for his coat. "Thank you for the cookies," he said with a warm smile. "And in particular, for the conversation. I didn't realize how much I needed that."

"I'm glad you stopped by to visit," Julie replied, her voice warm. "It has been years since I have shared such simple joy with someone. I feel so much better now. You're welcome to come over anytime."

He paused at the door, his hand resting on the knob. "Next time, I'll bring some of my sculptures... if you would like."

"I'd love that," Julie said, her smile widening.

As Robert stepped outside, he felt the frosty night air on his face, but spending time with Julie lingered in his heart. The snow crunched beneath his boots as he made his way back to his cabin, his thoughts filled with the unexpected connection he found with Julie.

Robert stoked the fire in his cabin, watching the flames dance in the hearth. The cabin felt very different from Julie's cabin since it was barren of decorations or anything homey. He hadn't planned on opening up to anyone during this trip, but somehow, talking to Julie made it easy. Her understanding, their shared experiences—he felt like he'd found someone who truly understood his pain.

He glanced at the unfinished sculptures on the table, thinking about their conversation. Robert felt a spark of hope for the first time in two years—hope that he didn't have to carry his grief alone.

New Horizons

5 Days before Christmas

THE MORNING SNOW BLANKETED the still lake, reflecting the muted winter light. Julie admired its serene beauty. The Christmas tree glowed in the corner, casting a warm glow over the room and creating an atmosphere of peacefulness she hadn't felt in years. This holiday season felt like a renewal of her heart. Something fresh was arising—a feeling of serenity and a touch of optimism.

She hadn't anticipated how easily she would slip into the quiet rhythm of life by the lake. Even more surprising was how her connection with Robert had grown, though they hadn't talked about it explicitly. The walls she built around herself were coming down, piece by piece. Though Julie hadn't fully let Robert in, she sensed her grip on grief loosening.

Julie finished her tea while thinking about Robert. His presence became an unexpected comfort, and though she grew accustomed to being alone, she looked forward to seeing him each day. There was something about him—steady, kind, but also carrying his own pain. She felt the pain he was dealing with, a sadness familiar to her working through the loss of her husband. Perhaps that was why she felt at ease around him. They carried similar scars, the unspoken pain of loss that hung between them like a shared secret.

A gentle knock at the door caused her to smile, expecting it to be Robert. She set her mug on the table and crossed the room to let him in. As expected, he stood there, cheeks flushed from the cold, his expression soft and familiar.

"I hope I'm not interrupting," he said, stepping inside as Julie waved him in. As he entered the cabin, the warm scent of cookies and the crackling fire greeted Robert, wrapping him in a familiar comfort.

"Not at all," Julie replied. "Come in and warm up." She motioned toward the fireplace, the flames flickering brightly.

Robert smiled as Julie was eyeing the large, closed cardboard box in his hands. He placed the box down on the table next to a chair in the living room. Pulling off his gloves, he rubbed his hands together to shake off the chill. "I have some of my sculptures to show you," he said. He reached inside the box and pulled out a small, detailed carving of a wooden bird.

Julie gasped as she took the sculpture in her hands. It was a bird looking up in flight; its wings spread wide as if soaring through the sky. Every delicate detail of the bird was etched into the wood, from the feathers on its wings to the graceful curve of its body and the determination on its face. She traced her fingers over the smooth surface, admiring the craftsmanship. "Robert, this is beautiful," as her eyes met his. "I am amazed at the detail."

He nodded, his expression thoughtful, "I started carving it not long after Lexi... after she passed. Birds meant a lot to her. She always said they symbolized freedom. I never could finish it until now."

Julie looked at him, her heart aching for the grief he still carried. Lexi's loss clung to his words, raw and heavy, feeling how much this carving meant to him. "Thank you for sharing this with me," she said. "I can imagine how hard it must have been to share it with me."

Robert's eyes lingered on the sculpture before shifting to the fire. "It is hard," he admitted in a low voice. "But being here... being with you... it feels like its time. Time to stop holding on so tightly."

They stood in silence. The connection between them felt as if they had been holding space for the right person, and now, that space was being filled, unexpectedly and beautifully. There was something fragile yet profound in the connection they shared. Both of them were holding back, waiting for the right opportunity to let someone in, and now it had come, leaving them both surprised.

Julie focused on the small table by the window. Robert had placed several other sculptures on the table for her to see. A rough-hewn piece immediately attracted her interest. She smiled, seeing not just art but Robert's reflection in each piece, which gave each sculpture a deeper meaning. She continued to look over each piece on the table.

"Tell me more about this rough piece," she said, pointing toward the sculpture. "You said it was something you'd been working on for a while, but it feels like there's more to it."

Robert's expression grew serious. "That is true. Carving has always been a way for me to process things. It's become how I deal with... so much now."

"It shows. The detail, the emotion—it's all there. Your work has a lot of heart, Robert. People would appreciate the depth of your work more than you know."

Robert shifted in his seat, uncomfortable with the praise. "I don't know about that. I've kept my work to myself. It is my expression from within for each piece. There wasn't a thought in my mind of showing them to others or to sell."

"You owe it to yourself and Lexi to share your work. It tells a story that others are looking for."

She paused. "Robert, would you let me put one of your sculptures on my website to see how it would be received?" *Her mind was already processing how she would display his sculptures.* "People can comment and vote to show more or not. You can choose the one we use. We don't have to list it for sale, and we can see if viewers are interested on the website."

"As long as it isn't for sale." He said firmly. With hesitation, he viewed the different sculptures on the table and chose what he called 'Flight Interrupted.' "This was a wooden sculpture Lexi started. She created the head and body of the bird with its right wing stretched out, angled up to the heavens, showing strength and vibrancy. After her death, I finished the bird with a broken left wing, rough and lifeless, signifying loss and the struggle to go higher while in pain from the broken wing."

Julie agreed to put a picture of 'Flight Interrupted' on her website, not for sale, but for comment and vote on whether to offer this type of work for sale. "I've got ideas for how we can set up a proper gallery on the website, and maybe we could even consider hosting an exhibit at the art gallery. We can discuss that later though, just a thought for now." They took a break as Robert needed to clear his mind. "Julie, would you like to go outside for a little bit? "Yes, I would. I need to bring some cookies over to the Riley's for the children. Let me place them in a decorative bag with a note for them. We can drop it off as part of our walk!"

They put on their coats, hats, scarves, and gloves. Julie grabbed the bag of cookies, and they walked over to the Riley's.

Robert enjoyed the cool, brisk breeze as Julie wrapped her scarf tighter around her to break the cold against her face.

Arriving at the Riley's, Julie knocked on the door. When there was no answer, they left the cookies on the porch by the door with a note.

They left Riley's cabin and went down to the edge of the lake, enjoying the scenery. Robert scooped up some snow and made a snowball. He tossed the snowball out into the lake and watched it land and break apart.

"I can't remember the last time I made a snowball!" Julie quipped, muffled by the scarf.

"It's fun, Julie. Reach down and make one!"

Julie bent down to the ground, mounded some snow, and made a snowball. She enjoyed that the snow was just right to make a well-built snowball. Memories of her childhood days when she played in the snow came to her mind. She drew her arm back, snowball in hand, and launched into the frozen lake. Like Robert's snowball, hers, too, hit the ice and broke apart.

They shared a laugh, enjoying the outdoors and playing in the snow.

"Shall we head back to the cabin?" Julie asked. "My hands are getting too cold."

"Sure, we had a fun outing. Let's get back. Can we have hot chocolate and cookies?"

"Yes, but we need to eat something better today, too. I have some split pea soup we can enjoy. Would you like to have some later?"

"Yes, that sounds like a wonderful dinner to have tonight, Julie."

They removed their winter gear after arriving at the cabin and Julie prepared the hot chocolate, while Robert grabbed a couple of plates, placing a few cookies on each.

Julie poured the hot chocolate into mugs, added whipped cream, cinnamon, and sprinkles, and brought them to the kitchen table. Together, they enjoyed their hot chocolate and cookies snack. "This is fantastic hot chocolate. This is a whole new experience for me, Julie."

Julie smiled. "That's because this is good hot chocolate. I also added some cardamom, which made it very enjoyable. I'm glad you like it."

Robert cleaned up after their snack while Julie went to a side bedroom to work on adding the 'Flight Interrupted' sculpture image to her website. She loaded the image onto the website, adding a poll for visitors to vote on their interest in sculptures to the gallery's collection, along with a place for comments.

Julie came back to the living room after working for a while on her website, finding Robert was resting. Julie rested, too.

Robert woke up and checked his watch. Seeing the time, he got up to move around. Julie got up as well, noting the time. She prepared the split pea soup and added slices of sourdough bread from the supermarket bakery to enjoy with the soup for dinner.

"This place is smelling wonderful from the soup you have on the stove!"

Julie turned, seeing him standing next to the kitchen table.

Robert sat down. "Yup, I just love this wonderful smell."

"I posted your 'Flight Interrupted' sculpture on my website."

Robert's eyes widened, surprise flickering across his face. "It is?"

"Yes, so let's give it some time and see how it is received by visitors to the website."

Julie brought over two warm bowls of split pea soup, along with pieces of sourdough bread.

As they ate, Julie shared some information about the website to familiarize Robert with how it worked, and that they would look at the site together tomorrow.

Robert commented on how much he enjoyed the soup, especially with the sourdough bread.

They finished their dinner, and Robert helped clean up. Then, they went to the living room and talked about things they had done when they were young.

And though neither of them said it aloud, they both knew that something had shifted. Something beautiful had taken root between them. Their time together felt natural, filled with peaceful silences and conversations when they walked around the lake, lowering the walls they had built around themselves. Their hearts were fragile but full of potential, and though they just met, there was hope. A shared understanding that they didn't have to face the future alone.

Realizing the time, Robert said he would go back to his cabin and start a new day tomorrow. They said goodnight, and Robert went out into the cold and walked to his cabin. The place was dark but warmed by the still-burning fire. He added a log for the night and got ready for bed. Thoughts and ideas about the website filled his mind, eager to see what the receptivity of his sculpting would be.

⤜⤜ ⤛⤛

The snow continued to fall outside as the fire crackled. Julie glanced once more at the wooden bird resting on the table. It was a symbol of hope, of freedom, of the healing she and Robert were both finding in each other's company. She felt ready to embrace the possibility of joy, to let go of the past—not the memories, but the grief.

She smiled to herself, her heart lighter than it had been in years. Whatever the future held, she knew she wasn't alone anymore. And for now, that was enough.

Building Trust

4 Days before Christmas

JULIE DREW BACK THE curtains, inviting the morning light to flood the room. The snow outside sparkled beneath the sunlight, a breathtaking reminder of winter's serene beauty. Beyond the glass, the world lay still, but Julie felt a worry she couldn't shake. *Things with Robert seemed to be moving quickly. Was it too soon, or was it the effect of years spent alone?* The morning's peace felt different—unsettling in its unfamiliarity.

Then there was a knock at the door. She shook off her worry and smiled, already knowing who it was. Julie opened the door, and Robert was there, his breath visible in the crisp air.

"Good morning," he said softly, his voice warm but subdued.

"Good morning," Julie replied with a smile. "Come on in."

Robert stepped inside. As he entered the cabin, the inviting scent of freshly brewed coffee welcomed him, instantly making him feel at home. Walking over to the fireplace, he added the log in his arms to the fire, stoking it to move the other logs around. He let the fire warm his hands once it got going again.

"I was thinking," Julie said as she poured him a cup of coffee, "how about we bake some more cookies today? Yesterday's batch didn't last long enough since most of them went to the Riley children."

Robert chuckled, accepting the mug with a grateful smile. "Sounds like a good idea. I could go for something sweet right about now, so let's make the next batch."

They moved into the kitchen, their movements synchronized and easy, as if they had been doing this together for years. The silence between them was comfortable, filled with the quiet sound of mixing ingredients and the gentle crackling of the fire in the background. Julie handed him the flour, and he began stirring, a soft smile playing on his lips as he worked.

As the cookies baked, Julie noticed that Robert seemed more introspective than usual. He sat at the table, staring into his coffee mug, his thoughts elsewhere. She sensed that something was weighing on him, something he wasn't quite ready to talk about.

"You're awfully quiet this morning," Julie said, sitting down across from him. "Is something on your mind?"

Robert looked up, meeting her gaze before sighing and leaning back in his chair. "Yeah, I guess there is," he admitted. "I've been thinking about the sculptures... and about selling them."

Julie set her coffee mug down, giving him her full attention. She had sensed that this might be on his mind. They talked more about his art, and though Robert knew she had put one of his pieces on her website, she knew it hadn't been an easy decision for him.

"I know it's a big step," Julie said, her voice calm and understanding. "Don't rush into anything if you're not ready."

"I'm not sure how I feel about putting that part of myself out there for strangers to judge. It's just... carving has been personal for me. It's how I process things going on inside of me I don't know how to express."

Julie nodded, understanding his hesitation. "I get that," she said. "But your work has meaning, Robert. It's not just about selling a carved piece of wood—it's about sharing a part of yourself and maybe even helping someone else find a little healing through your art. That's something special."

Robert was silent, his gaze drifting toward the window. "I don't know if I'm ready for that," he admitted quietly.

"There is no need to decide right now," she said softly. "But when you're ready, I'm here to help." Julie put her hand on his arm.

Robert glanced at her, his expression easing just a little. "Thanks," he murmured. "I just... I don't want to lose the meaning behind it. The carving holds a special meaning for me. I'm not sure I can handle people interpreting my sculptures in ways I didn't intend."

Julie smiled, her hand resting on his arm. "That's the beauty of art, though. Once you put it out into the world, it takes on a life of its own. People will see what they see in it from their life perspective. But that doesn't take away from what it means to you. It just adds another layer."

Robert let out a soft sigh, but it wasn't as heavy this time. He seemed to be considering her words, how it all was making sense in his mind. After a moment, he looked back at her and offered an appreciative smile.

Julie chuckled, withdrawing her hand from his arm. "I'm just speaking from my experience," she said. "I've been where you are—feeling like my art was too personal to share. But I realized it didn't lose its meaning for me. If anything, it became even more meaningful because of what it meant to other people."

Robert remained deep in thought. A couple of minutes later, hoping to ease the heaviness, Julie changed the subject.

"Why don't I show you how the website works?" she suggested. "That way, you can see how your pieces would be displayed and how we can make sure they are presented in a way that feels right to you."

Robert seemed to relax a little at the suggestion. "Yeah, I'd like that," he said, his voice soft but more at ease.

Julie grabbed her laptop from the counter, opened it up at the table, and went to her art gallery's website page. The website, called **Art Brings Healing Gallery,** reflected her journey with grief and healing through her own work. The design was simple yet elegant, with sections dedicated to different forms of art—paintings, and photography among them, hoping to add sculptures next.

"This is where your sculpture is listed," Julie said, pointing to the image of his piece 'Flight Interrupted.' "I added some description, but we can adjust anything you want. The people who visit this site aren't just looking for paintings. They're searching for art with meaning, something that resonates with them."

Robert leaned in to get a better look, and Julie could see him relax as he studied the layout. "It looks good," he admitted. "Better than I expected."

"Here is where the viewer comments are, Robert! Have a look. There are 39 comments so far, and the poll results favor adding sculptures to the website at 84%! What do you think about that, Robert?"

Robert looked at the web info, seeing what Julie shared. They read over all the comments and each one loved the sculpture, 'Flight Interrupted,' and had many ways of appreciating the sculpture of the bird with a broken wing. "I feel so much better about this, Julie. I do better understand now what you said about allowing other people to have their own experience with a piece of sculpture."

Julie smiled, relieved that he was warming up to the idea. "I told you, people are going to love your work."

Robert seemed to take that in, feeling a mix of hope and apprehension. "I can see how this could work."

Relief settled over Julie. She didn't want to push him, but she knew how important it was for Robert to take this step—not just for his art, but for his own healing.

"How about a break?" Julie felt he needed to clear his mind. "A walk by the lake might help clear your head."

Robert looked up at her and nodded, a small smile returning to his face. "Yeah, that sounds good."

They bundled up and stepped outside, the cold air biting at their cheeks as they walked toward the lake. The snow crunched beneath their boots, and the landscape stretched out before them. A pristine expanse of white, interrupted only by the bare trees and the distant line of the forest.

As they reached the edge of the lake, Julie stopped, taking in the beauty of the frozen water. "This place... it's always felt like a sanctuary to me," she said softly. "Whenever I needed space to think or just breathe, I came here."

Robert stood beside her, looking at the large frozen lake. "I can feel the peace here as well."

Julie nodded, her eyes scanning the landscape. "After Ted passed, this was where I came to process everything. It wasn't just about escaping—it was about finding a way to heal. The quiet, the solitude... it gave me the space to feel what I needed to feel."

Robert was silent for a long moment, then spoke in a voice heavy with emotion. "I've been thinking a lot about Lexi. Christmas was her favorite holiday," he admitted. "About how much I've been holding onto the guilt. Coming here, being around you... it's made me realize that maybe it's time to start letting go."

Julie turned to him, her heart aching for what he still carried. "It's a process," she said. "Just take it one step at a time."

Robert glanced at her, his expression softening. "Thanks," he whispered. "For everything."

They stood together, listening to the sound of the wind blowing through the trees and the distant call of a bird.

As they continued their walk, the conversation shifted to lighter topics. They discussed the art gallery and the possibility of showcasing Robert's work.

They shared a quiet smile, and as they walked back toward their cabins, Julie felt hope for the future—both for herself and for Robert. The walk had brought them closer, not just physically, but emotionally. Though they both still had a way to go, Julie was certain they would face whatever came next together.

Back at Julie's cabin, they settled by the fire once again, releasing the last of the chill from their walk. Robert sat beside her, his gaze thoughtful as he stared into the flames.

"I think I'm finally ready," he said softly. "To move forward."

"You are not alone," Julie said, her heart full of understanding.

Robert turned to her, his eyes filled with gratitude. "I know that now!"

The fire crackled in the background, and as they sat together, his mind relaxed and soon was replaced by trust. They didn't need to say anything more. The bond they were building, though still fragile, was growing stronger with each passing day.

Test of Tensions

4 Days before Christmas

JULIE WAS PREPARING TO show Robert more about her website after they had both rested from their walk around the lake. The afternoon was calm and peaceful, and the fire crackled as warmth filled the cabin. They had spent some time enjoying each other's company, and Julie felt like things were starting to fall into place. She was smiling and about to ask Robert a question.

A sharp knock at the door interrupted the tranquility, pulling each of them from their thoughts.

Surprise mixed with confusion appeared on Julie's face. No one was expected, and she hadn't heard anyone approach. She saw two women through the peephole and pulled the door open, to be unkindly greeted by two women standing on her porch. The taller woman had a familiar face—Julie recognized her from a photo Robert had shown her.

"Bonnie?" Julie said with uncertainty and looked back at Robert. He recognized the voices and got up from his seat as his body tensed up.

Julie didn't know what to expect, and it didn't start out well.

"Bonnie... Rachel?" Robert's voice was tight as he moved toward the door. His expression shifted into one of heightened stress. Without a word, he stepped outside onto the patio, motioning for Julie to stay back as he closed the door behind him.

Bonnie, the woman who had survived the car accident that took her daughter Robin's life and Lexi's as well—offered a hesitant smile. Rachel, Robert's ex-wife, stood stiffly beside her. Her face was colder, her eyes clouded with unresolved anger.

"We *happened* to be in the area," Rachel said, her tone sharp. "I heard you came up here for Christmas. When you weren't at the cabin, we followed your footprints here." Her eyes swept over the porch, lingering on Julie's decorations before settling back on Robert.

"Didn't expect to find you... *so cozy*," Rachel added, her words cutting through the air with an edge that made Julie wince from inside. "I don't know if you've moved on or if you're just pretending," Rachel said, her voice hard but her eyes glistening. "I just... I hope you're okay, even if I can't be."

Inside the cabin, Julie could hear every word, though it felt as if she shouldn't be listening in on the conversation. The exchange outside was thick, making her stomach churn with unease. Rachel's tone carried a bitterness that sent a chill through her. She couldn't recall a time when she had heard such bitterness. The resentment that Julie felt was aimed not only at Robert but indirectly at her, too.

Robert's jaw tightened as he spoke, his voice firm but strained. "What are you doing here?"

Bonnie became uncomfortable. "We just wanted to check on you, Robert. See how you're doing. It's been a while."

Rachel's gaze flicked between Robert and the cozy cabin behind him, her lips curling into a tight, accusatory smile. "Seems like you've moved on just fine," she said, her voice dripping with sarcasm.

Still standing near the door, Julie felt her discomfort increase. Rachel's harsh words weren't aimed directly at her, but they carried enough venom that she could feel their sting. She wondered how Robert would respond, knowing that the battle between him and his past was far from resolved.

"Rachel, don't," Robert warned, his voice taking on a sharper edge, though the tension in his body betrayed the calmness he was trying to maintain.

Bonnie attempted to calm down Rachel. The attempt didn't go longer than a minute. "Maybe this isn't the time and place for this," Rachel said.

Then Rachel's eyes narrowed as she took a step closer to him, her anger not contained. "**Two years**, Robert. Two years since Lexi died, and *this* is where you are?" Rachel's voice cracked mid-sentence. For a moment, she looked away as if searching for something she'd lost long before. When she turned back, her expression hardened again, masking whatever vulnerability had surfaced.

Her words hit like a hammer, and Julie's heart clenched in response. She didn't know the full story between Robert and Rachel, but the pain and bitterness she felt told her enough.

Sensing the brewing storm, Bonnie stepped forward, her voice trembling with emotion. "Rachel, please. We didn't come here to fight."

But it was too late. The conversation had already spiraled into a conflict that had been simmering for years. Rachel's bitterness was palpable, her words laced with accusations that had long been held back. She crossed her arms around her, then dropped them as if holding herself together had become too much. She bit her lip, her eyes darting between Robert and the snow-covered floor of the patio.

"Maybe if you paid attention to me, and instead of hiding in your *sculpting*, you would've noticed what was happening to us," Rachel snapped. Her voice trembling with emotion, her hands clenched at her sides. "I remember the Christmases when we laughed as a family," Rachel said, her tone bitter but her eyes softening for a moment. "Lexi insisted on putting the star on top of the tree, even though she could barely reach. Those moments... they're gone now." She swallowed hard, and the anger returned with a vengeance, sharper than before. "Maybe I'm just... grasping at blame," Rachel muttered inaudibly. "But I don't know how else to deal with this, Robert." She shook her head, her shoulders rigid once more.

Robert's face darkened, his hands curling into fists at his sides. "Don't you **dare** put this all on me, Rachel. We **both** know what happened."

Inside, Julie sat down at the kitchen table, her hands folded in her lap as she listened to the heated exchange. She didn't want to intrude, but the heaviness in the room was suffocating, pressing down on her with every word spoken outside. Her heart ached for Robert, knowing how much pain this conversation must be stirring up for him.

"Maybe it's better this way," Rachel continued, her voice sharp and bitter. "At least now it's *obvious* to me that you've moved on."

Robert's voice dropped lower, tight with barely controlled anger. "Rachel, this *isn't the time* for this."

Bonnie stepped forward again, still trying to keep the peace, her voice calm but pleading. "Rachel, let it go. We didn't come here to have this fight."

Rachel crossed her arms with frustration evident in every part of her body. "Fine. Let's just go.""I'm sorry *your friend* had to hear this," Rachel said, glancing at the window with an expression that held a mix of apology and bitterness. "I didn't mean to intrude on... whatever this is."

Without another word, she turned and stormed off the porch, her footsteps crunching angrily in the snow. Bonnie lingered behind, her gaze flicking between Robert and the path where Rachel had disappeared. After a brief hesitation, she followed her friend down the steps toward the car.

Inside, Julie remained seated at the table, her fingers tracing the edge of the tablecloth absently as she tried to process what had just unfolded. She felt an overwhelming sadness, both for Robert and for what had been lost in his life. The weight of his past had come crashing into their peaceful afternoon like a storm, and Julie knew that he hadn't been prepared for it.

The sound of the front door closing quietly behind Robert took her out of her thoughts. He stood there, his hand still on the doorknob as if he needed a moment to collect himself before turning back to face her.

Outside, the sun was beginning to set, casting long shadows over the snow-covered landscape. The sky had taken on a deep violet hue, the last light of day slipping away.

"I'm sorry you had to overhear that," Robert said, his voice rough with emotion as he stepped further into the room. His gaze was fixed on the floor, his shoulders slumped after dealing with the confrontation.

Julie shook her head. "No apology needed, Robert. These things can get... complicated. Rachel is hurting and needs help beyond what she is doing now."

Robert sighed deeply, moving to stand by the fire. The flames flickered, casting long, dancing shadows across the walls, but the warmth from the hearth did little to ease the thoughts that hung between them. "It's just... so messy," he admitted. "Rachel and I never dealt with Lexi's death. We couldn't. Every time we tried, it just turned into blame and anger. And Bonnie... she was there when it happened. She went through so much recovering from the accident, then finding out that Robin and Lexi didn't survive. I still don't know how to understand any of it."

Julie stood and moved closer to him, her voice soft with understanding. "There is no need to explain everything right now," she said. "I get it, and I will help you through this."

Robert turned to her, and the raw pain in his eyes made Julie's chest tighten. "I didn't want you to see this part of my life. It's not... it's not something I'm proud of."

"We all carry things, Robert," Julie said. "It's okay. Grief is grief. We all experience it differently. You can open up to me."

The tension eased, but Julie knew that Robert's wounds were far from healed. Walls remained barriers that would take time to break down. But for now, she was willing to stand by him and offer her quiet support as he navigated the difficult emotions that had been stirred up.

There was little solace from the emotional storm they had just weathered, but it was enough to offer a small measure of comfort.

Outside, the snow began to fall again as the sun dipped below the horizon, leaving the world in a hushed, frozen stillness.

Moments of Distance

3 Days before Christmas

YESTERDAY'S CONFRONTATION WITH ROBERT, Rachel, and Bonnie lingered as Julie looked out at the peace of the frozen lake. The unresolved tension conflicted with the stillness outside. How could she ease the chill of those heated words and emotions? Since their visit, Robert had grown more withdrawn, his silence creating a barrier. When he retreated to his cabin, he left Julie feeling the raw emotions in her mind.

Julie poured herself a cup of fresh coffee and took a sip. She recalled how the distant, heavy look in his eyes when he left had stayed with her. Their time at the lake had been shattered by Rachel and Bonnie's arrival. But now that it had happened, Julie wasn't sure how to confront the confused feelings stirring within her.

Outside, the snow-covered lake shimmered under the pale winter sun, its beauty serene yet cold. Julie couldn't help but feel uneasy, as though the stillness of the landscape mirrored the growing distance between her and Robert.

A knock at the door interrupted her thoughts. Glancing at the clock, Julie noted that it was still early. She set her mug down on the kitchen counter and opened the door, seeing Robert standing there.

"Hey," he said softly, his voice heavy with fatigue.

"Hey, come on in." Robert removed his coat, though the stress for him was still noticeable.

Robert was quiet. Julie motioned toward the coffeepot. "Coffee?"

Robert nodded, seemingly grateful for the offer. "Yeah, thanks. That'd be great."

As Julie poured the coffee, she could feel his eyes on her, though he remained silent. She handed him the mug, and he wrapped his hands around it, holding it tightly as if trying to absorb the warmth.

"How'd you sleep last night?" Julie asked, breaking the silence, though she already expected his answer.

Robert shrugged, his expression unreadable. "Not well. I... I was thinking."

Julie leaned against the counter, her arms folded across her chest as she watched him. "About yesterday?"

Robert's jaw tightened, and he gave a short nod. "Yeah. About a lot of things."

Their conversation from yesterday was still lingering. Julie could sense that Robert wasn't ready to open up, but the silence between them felt heavy, as though they were both waiting for something to break.

"I'm sorry you had to witness that," Robert said, his voice heavy with regret. "It wasn't fair to you."

Julie shook her head. "Don't apologize, Robert. Things like this happen."

"I'm not sure how to explain it all," Robert admitted, looking at the coffee mug in his hands. "Everything with Lexi and Rachel... it's just so complicated. Letting go of the past isn't as easy as I thought it would be."

Julie's heart ached for him. "This is not something that goes away," she said. "It takes time."

Robert looked up at her, his expression softening, but there was still concern in his eyes. "I'm tired of carrying this pain."

Julie felt a tightness in her chest at his words, but she didn't push him. Instead, she took a step closer, offering him a quiet reassurance. "You are dealing with your pain. It's a process to work through," she said softly.

Robert didn't respond right away, but she could see he was working through his feelings. He took another sip of his coffee, his movements slow, as if trying to buy himself more time to think.

After a long moment of silence, Julie spoke again, hoping to ease his concern. "How about a walk? The lake looks beautiful this morning, and I think we could both use some fresh air."

Robert hesitated. He looked over through the window. "Yeah. A walk sounds good."

They walked in silence, hearing each other's footsteps as they crossed the snow. The cold air reflected the distance they were trying to bridge.

Outside, the air was crisp and biting, their breath visible as they walked along the snow-covered path that led toward the lake. The snow crunched under their boots, the only sound breaking the quiet stillness of the world around them.

Julie glanced at Robert as they walked, sensing the pressure in his posture but not wanting to push him to talk. Instead, they walked in companionable silence, the cold air sharp but invigorating.

Robert noticed a bright red cardinal landing on a nearby tree branch. He points to it, getting Julie's attention and sharing their enjoyment of its beautiful coloring and cheeriness. This brightened both of their moods.

"I remember being at places like this with Lexi," Robert said. "We'd have fun every Christmas together."

Julie took a moment to respond, letting his words settle between them. She could hear the pain in his voice, from his memories. "Hold on to those happy memories, Robert," Julie said, her voice soft.

"I will," with a small, wistful smile. "She often said Christmas made her feel free, like nothing could hold her back."

Julie smiled. "She sounds like she was an incredible young lady."

"She was," Robert agreed. "And that's what makes it so hard. I don't know how to move on without feeling like I'm betraying her."

Julie stopped walking, turning to face him. "You're not betraying her, Robert," she said firmly. "You're honoring her by living your life. By sharing your art with the world."

Robert looked at her, his eyes filled with uncertainty. "I don't know if I'm ready for that yet."

Julie reached out, placing her hand on his arm. "It's okay if you're not ready yet. But when you are, you'll know. And I'll be here."

They stood there as the snow fell around them. His burden hadn't disappeared, but there was an understanding, a promise that they wouldn't face the future alone.

Later that evening, they sat by the fire in Julie's cabin, the warmth from the flames easing the chill from their walk. Robert stared into the fire, his thoughts still heavy, but there was a softness to his expression now, a hint of peace that hadn't been there before.

"Thank you for listening. For understanding."

Julie smiled. "I know how hard it is to open up about this kind of pain. But I'm glad you did. It isn't good to keep it building inside of you. I learned the hard way and can show you how to work through your pain."

As the evening set in, the stars twinkled outside. Robert turned to Julie with a thoughtful expression. "You know, I've been thinking about what you said yesterday. About showcasing my sculptures at your art gallery."

Julie looked at him, her curiosity piqued. "Oh? Have you decided to take me up on my offer?"

Robert hesitated. "Yeah. I think I'm ready. It's time to stop hiding behind my grief and start sharing something positive with the world."

Julie's smile widened, her heart lifting at his words. "I think that's a wonderful decision, Robert. Your work should be seen to help others heal."

Robert looked down at his hands, his expression still thoughtful. "It feels strange, though. Like I'm moving on from Lexi in some way."

"You're not moving on from her," Julie said. "You're honoring her memory in a way that keeps her spirit alive. Sharing your sculptures doesn't mean you're forgetting her. It means you're keeping her close in a better way."

Robert nodded, her words resonating with him. "I think you're right," he said quietly. "It's just... hard."

"I know. Take your time. When you're ready, I'll be there to help."

As the evening continued, their conversation shifted to lighter topics, and their bond deepened with each passing moment. By the time they parted ways for the night, they felt a new sense of peace that had eluded them for far too long.

As Julie settled into bed, her thoughts drifted to Robert and the connection they were building. She hadn't expected to find someone who understood her grief so deeply. Robert made her feel like it was okay to let go of the past and embrace the future. She saw her future as to reach for, not something to fear.

Opening Old Wounds

2 Days before Christmas

THE SNOW STOPPED FALLING by the time Robert and Julie finished their breakfast. Though the storm had passed, the intense confrontation from the other day still lingered in Robert's mind. Julie studied Robert's quiet demeanor across the table. His body looked rigid, and his eyes clouded from all the memories he wasn't ready to share.

"Would you like to take a walk around the lake?" Julie asked, hoping to break his thoughts. The fresh blanket of snow outside had always had a calming effect on her.

"Yeah, that sounds good to me."

They bundled up and stepped outside. The cold air hit their faces as they followed the path toward the lake. The frozen surface stretched out before them, smooth and untouched by the snowfall. They walked side by side, their boots crunching in the snow. The silence between them no longer felt uncomfortable, but it was laden with things unsaid.

As they neared a small bench overlooking the lake, Robert stopped, staring out over the icy water. His breath fogged in the cold air, and Julie could see that something weighed on his mind.

"Robert?" she asked, stopping beside him. "Is something bothering you?"

He didn't answer immediately, his gaze fixed on the distant horizon. After a long pause, he spoke. "I've been thinking about what you said yesterday. About forgiveness." His voice was quiet, almost fragile. "I've carried this guilt for so long... I'm not sure I know how to let it go."

Julie nodded, her heart aching for him. She understood too well how grief could turn into guilt, making one believe they were responsible for things beyond their control. She reached out, took his hand, and offered silent comfort.

"It's okay to take your time," she said softly. "Forgiveness, especially self-forgiveness, isn't something that has to happen overnight."

Robert glanced down at their joined hands, his brow furrowed with conflicted thoughts. "I blamed Bonnie and Rachel for what happened to Lexi," he admitted, his voice thick with emotion. "I said things I shouldn't have, but part of me still holds them responsible, even though I know it was a terrible accident. It wasn't either of their faults. I don't know how to move past that."

Julie squeezed his hand, her empathy deepening. "Grief can make us feel things we don't want to feel. But holding onto that blame won't bring Lexi back, and it won't bring peace."

Robert sighed, the pain in his eyes unmistakable. "I know you're right," he said quietly, "but every time I think I'm getting closer to making peace with it, something drags me back."

Julie thought of Ted and the moments when her own grief had resurfaced unexpectedly. She had experienced the same struggle—how the pain could return in waves, as fresh as the day it had first struck. She knew how hard it was to find a way through it.

"After Ted died, I blamed myself, wondering if I could have done something. It took years to accept it wasn't my fault. Sometimes... things happen, and there's nothing we can do to change them."

Robert looked at her, his expression thoughtful. "How did you move past it?" he asked, his voice barely a whisper.

Julie took a deep breath, her gaze drifting toward the icy lake. "I realized that holding onto guilt was keeping me stuck. It wasn't honoring Ted's memory—it was only hurting me. So, little by little, I started to let go. It didn't happen all at once, but over time, I learned to forgive myself. That's when I finally began to heal."

Robert was silent, absorbing her words for a few moments. "I'm not sure I'm ready to forgive myself."

"Just by saying it, I think you are, more than you'll admit," Julie replied. "Give yourself the space to forgive."

They continued walking along the lake toward her cabin, the cold air invigorating despite the heaviness of their conversation. By the time they returned to Julie's cabin, the sky had begun to darken, casting long shadows over the snow.

Inside, the fire was already crackling in the hearth, its warmth quickly chasing away the chill from outside. Julie went into the kitchen to make tea while Robert settled on the couch, staring into the flames with a faraway look in his eyes.

When she returned with two steaming mugs, she handed one to Robert and sat beside him, finding he had come to some resolve. The earlier tension had eased somewhat, replaced by a quiet understanding.

"Thank you for being here this year to help me through what has been trapped inside of me."

Julie smiled. "I'm just glad you're opening up. That is a good sign."

They sipped their tea, watching the fire flicker beside them, the warmth filling the room with a calming peace.

"I've got some frozen pizza in the freezer. Want that for dinner tonight?" Julie asked.

"Sounds perfect, Julie. Want me to get it started?"

"Let's do it together," she replied as they both headed to the kitchen.

Julie pulled out the frozen pizza, set the oven to 400 degrees, and grabbed a pizza pan from the cabinet. Unwrapping the cheese pizza, she placed it on the pan.

"Robert, could you get the oregano, basil, red pepper flakes, and olive oil? I'll grab the turkey pepperoni."

Julie drizzled a bit of olive oil on the pizza, then sprinkled the oregano, basil, and red pepper flakes before topping it off with turkey pepperoni. A couple of minutes later, the oven beeped, signaling it was ready. She set the timer for 14 minutes.

Meanwhile, Robert set the table with two plates and napkins, bringing their mugs of tea over from the counter.

When the pizza was ready, Julie took it out of the oven, letting it cool for a few moments. "I'll cut it into six slices," she said with a grin. "I don't think we're up for eight."

They both chuckled.

Sitting down, enjoying light conversation, they each took a slice, savoring the flavors with each bite. Six slices turned out to be just the right amount—they couldn't have agreed more.

"I enjoyed dinner tonight. Thank you, Julie."

"It was good, wasn't it?"

After cleaning up after dinner, they went outside for a few minutes while Robert grabbed a few more logs from the back. The bright stars were shining against the clear, dark sky. Then, they both went inside, and Robert placed the logs next to the fireplace.

⟶⟫⟩ ⟨⟪⟵

Later that evening, Robert turned to Julie with a thoughtful expression. "You know, I've been thinking more about exhibiting my sculptures at your art gallery."

Julie looked at him, intrigued. "Oh? What kind of thoughts?"

"Will you put some of your art in the exhibit so we can both have our creations on display?"

Julie's smile widened, her heart lifting at his words. "I am sure we can work that out. I think it's a wonderful idea."

"Then let's do it!"

Robert smiled as their conversation flowed a little longer, reflecting on happy memories. Both Robert and Julie felt lighter in spirit with an increased sense of healing.

The time was late. Julie was ready to get some rest and was happy that Robert had agreed to exhibit his sculptures.

Robert knew it was time to go back to his cabin for the night.

They said their goodbyes. Julie watched Robert walk over to his cabin as she closed the door and got ready for bed.

When Robert returned to his cabin, he fixed the fire for the night and sat in his chair with the light shining on one of his sculptures. He reflected on all that has happened since he arrived. A smile came to him, realizing he was healing and beginning to feel much better.

Robert hasn't been able to sleep well for years. Julie helped him realize that all the guilt and what ifs only held *him* back. Now that he was able to relax, he turned out the light and went to sleep.

Path to Healing

Christmas Eve Day

In silence, Robert drove back to his cabin, reflecting on his rocky meeting with Rachel earlier—her surprise call was an invitation to meet up and talk. After years of emotional distance and unresolved pain, they were able to speak with each other and resolve many of their issues. They both agreed to visit Lexi's grave together. They stood together, sharing the emotion-filled time, which brought closure and relief to Rachel and Robert.

His drive back to the lake felt peaceful, almost soothing. Silence during the drive was interrupted by the crunch of the tires against the snow-covered road as Robert's thoughts wandered. The lavender sky of dusk mingled with the twinkling lights from distant homes, casting a serene glow over the frozen landscape.

As he turned onto the road leading back to the lake, Julie's cabin came into view. The warm glow from the decorated windows beckoned him, the twinkling Christmas lights reflecting off the snow, inviting him back into the cozy refuge. It felt like returning to a different world—one filled with warmth, peace, and the promise of something new. The warmth of Julie's cabin was a stark contrast to what he had weathered earlier in the day with Rachel.

Stepping out of the car, he was confronted by the chilly evening air, but there was undeniable comfort in knowing that Julie was waiting inside. He knocked on the door, and when she answered, her soft and welcoming smile was a balm to his weary soul.

"You're back." She said.

"I am, and happily so," Robert replied as he entered, feeling toasty warm. The cheery decorations enabled him to relax, the weight of the day slowly easing off his mind. "It's been a long day."

Julie didn't ask any questions; she simply led him to the kitchen table. "Come sit. I just made some tea. It is good to see you smile."

They sat at the kitchen table, sipping tea. Then Julie shared some Christmas cookies. Robert glanced around, appreciating the additional festive touches Julie had added. The table felt welcoming and homier than he had expected, and it soothed him in a way he hadn't realized he needed.

"This place feels like Christmas," Robert remarked, nodding toward the small tree in the corner. The branches were adorned with ornaments, and the lights twinkled. "You've brought the spirit of the season to life here."

Julie smiled, a mix of pride and nostalgia in her expression. "It's the first time I've decorated in years. At first, it felt strange, but now... it feels right. Like I'm finally ready to embrace Christmas again."

Robert nodded, his heart softening at her words. He knew exactly what she meant—the feeling of reclaiming something that had once been lost. "I went to see Rachel today," he said, his voice steady but reflective. "We talked about Lexi... about everything."

Julie's expression softened, her hand resting on his arm. "How did it go?"

"It was difficult," Robert admitted, his gaze distant. "But... it was necessary. We visited Lexi's grave together. It provided closure for both of us."

Julie squeezed his arm, her touch offering comfort without needing words. "I'm glad you could do that," she said softly. "Closure is important."

"There's more," Robert continued after a moment of reflection. "I left a letter for Bonnie. I wasn't ready to face her directly, but I needed to tell her I don't blame her for the accident anymore. I know she's been carrying that guilt, and I hope the letter helps her let go of some of it."

Julie's heart ached for the burden Bonnie must have been carrying over the years. "That was a brave thing to do," she whispered. "And kind."

"I don't know if it was brave," Robert replied, a small, tired smile tugging at his lips. "But it was time. I've held onto that anger for too long, and I needed to let it go."

"I feel so much better, as the pain I carried is being lifted off me, Julie."

They sat together in front of the fire, the silence comfortable and soothing. Their bond had deepened over the past few days, and at that moment, it felt as though they had crossed an invisible threshold. One where their pasts no longer defined them.

After finishing the tea and cookies, Robert stood and walked over to the small Christmas tree by the window.

They stood together, side by side, watching the lights twinkle on the tree. The air between them was filled with unspoken joy and hope. A promise of something new.

Robert glanced at Julie. "This is the first Christmas in years I have enjoyed," he admitted.

Julie smiled, her heart swelling with warmth. "Me too. It feels different this year. Lighter."

Robert's hand brushed against hers, the touch gentle but full of significance. "Thank you," he said quietly. "For everything. I am ready to enjoy Christmas!"

Julie's eyes met his, and in that moment, the connection between them felt undeniable. "I am glad to hear you say that. I think we've both helped each other more than we realize."

Robert and Julie exchanged quiet smiles as the fire crackled and the snow fell outside. The warmth of the moment gave them a peace they had both been searching for.

For Robert, this Christmas was the first in years that he didn't feel weighed down by the past. For Julie, it was a moment of renewal, a chance to embrace the future, no longer shackled by grief.

As the evening unfolded, their conversation continued. They talked about their hopes for the future, their dreams, and their fears, their laughter filling the space between. By the time the fire had burned down to embers, they both felt lighter, as though they had let go of the burdens they had carried for so long.

Later that night, as Julie settled into bed, she felt hopeful about what was to come. The future, once so uncertain, now seemed full of possibilities. With Robert by her side, she knew they would face whatever came next together.

Hearts Alight at Christmas

Christmas Day

"IT'S CHRISTMAS MORNING," JULIE said enthusiastically. She woke up early, excited to spend the whole day enjoying Christmas. She is expecting Robert to come over soon. After enjoying a pancake breakfast, they would prepare the Christmas dinner.

Julie prepared the pancake ingredients while the coffee brewed. A knock at the door interrupted her thoughts. Robert had arrived.

"Merry Christmas, Robert!"

"Merry Christmas to you, Julie."

"I'm making pancakes. Want to help?"

"Sure, let's get going. I am ready for some pancakes this morning."

They enjoyed their pancakes and coffee before tidying up and preparing for Christmas dinner.

Julie and Robert spent the early hours in her cabin preparing a festive meal together. The kitchen was alive with the rich aromas of their holiday meal. Creating fresh memories for themselves as the holiday spirit continues to bring them closer together.

For Julie, the standing rib roast in the oven and the pies cooling on the counter evoked a strange yet comforting sense of normalcy. She hadn't felt like this on Christmas in years. Memories of past holidays with Ted are now part of her new life. She focused on the present, on the joy of sharing the day with Robert as they created new Christmas memories together.

As she glanced at him, a new warmth spread through her chest. She hadn't expected this—the connection, the companionship. It felt right. Robert, too, seemed more at ease than she had seen him. The guarded expression he often wore was softer now, replaced with a lightness that hadn't been there before.

"I think we've outdone ourselves," Robert said, placing the last dish on the table, a satisfied smile tugging at his lips.

Julie grinned as she stood back to admire their handiwork. The table was beautifully set, adorned with festive napkins, candles, and an evergreen centerpiece she had created herself. The glow of the lights from the Christmas tree added a cozy warmth to the room, making everything feel just a little more magical.

"I think you're right," Julie replied, her eyes twinkling with shared excitement.

They sat down to eat, the atmosphere between them light, filled with laughter and the soft crackling of the fire. Their conversation flowed easily, punctuated by stories from past Christmases. Robert reminisced about the way Lexi insisted on decorating every inch of the house and used to sing Christmas carols off-key. Julie reflected on Ted's love for cooking holiday meals and how he would always sneak a taste of the turkey before it was ready, claiming it was for "quality control."

Though both of them still felt the memories of their losses, this Christmas was different. It was about embracing new beginnings and weaving in the memories of cherished loved ones. They were creating new traditions now, bringing a greater sense of healing.

"I can't remember the last time I laughed this much on Christmas," Robert said, his voice filled with a hint of surprise. He leaned back in his chair, looking around the room with appreciation, his eyes lingering on the twinkling tree and the fire. "It feels good to... to feel this way again."

Julie nodded, a soft smile touching her lips. "I know what you mean. For so long, Christmas was just a reminder of what I had lost. But this year... it feels like a new beginning."

Robert's eyes met hers, and neither of them spoke. There was a renewed understanding between them, a mutual understanding of the journeys they had been on. Their grief had lessened, replaced by the gentle promise of something more.

After dinner, they cleaned up the dishes and cookware used for the dinner together. The simple act of cleaning up felt like an extension of the rhythm they had fallen into—each movement comfortable, familiar. There was no need to rush, no pressure to fill the silence. It was enough to be together.

Once the kitchen was tidy, they returned to the living room, where the fire still glowed warmly. The tree in the corner sparkled with lights and smelling the rich aromas still present from their meal.

"How about we exchange gifts now?" Robert asked.

Robert handed Julie a small box wrapped in gold paper.

"Open it," he said, his voice gentle but filled with anticipation.

Julie unwrapped the gift, looking forward to receiving this gift. Inside was a beautifully crafted ornament, a delicate sculpture of a dove, its wings spread in graceful flight.

"It's from Lexi's collection," Robert said. "She made it during her last Christmas. It's always been a symbol of peace for me. I thought... I thought you might like it and that it brings peace to you, too."

Julie's eyes filled with gratitude as she cradled the delicate ornament, sensing the love and care that went into its creation.

"Thank you, Robert. This... this means more than you know. I am sure it was hard for you to give this to me. Know that I will always cherish this ornament."

"After everything we've discussed about the exhibit and the website, I wanted you to be the first to see it. I thought... maybe it could symbolize a new beginning. For both of us," he said.

Julie smiled through her tears, her heart full. "It's perfect. I am so happy to have this ornament."

In return, Julie handed Robert a gift she had been working on in her quiet moments at the cabin—a painting of the lake at sunrise. The colors were soft, the light just beginning to peek over the horizon, capturing the tranquility and promise of a new day.

Robert's eyes widened as he took in the painting, and his expression was filled with awe. He took a few minutes to study the detail in the picture, observing the tone and colors used to bring out its natural beauty. The cabins were dotted among the mature trees around the wonderful lake.

"This is incredible," he said. "You've captured the lake perfectly, and sunrise feels so real to me. This captures exactly how it feels to be here!"

"I wanted you to have something to remind you of this place... And... of us," Julie said.

Robert's eyes met hers, his voice soft with emotion. "Thank you, Julie. This means more than I can say."

They sat together by the fire. The lights on the tree and the flicker of the fire cast a golden glow over the room, creating an intimate atmosphere. For a while, they enjoyed the peace of the moment and the comfort of each other's presence.

"I never thought I'd feel this way again," Robert said after a long pause, his voice filled with sincerity. "I didn't think I'd be able to share Christmas with someone who understands, who makes everything feel... right."

"Neither did I," Julie replied, her heart swelling with the same sense of rightness. "But I'm glad we found each other."

Julie and Robert enjoyed listening to Christmas carols on the radio together. They sang some songs on occasion, blending with the soft crackling of the fire. It was the simple, joyful moments they hadn't planned but cherished deeply. They both felt the uncertainty ahead, but were ready to embrace whatever came next.

As the fire dwindled, Robert placed another log, watching the flames dance back to life. It was time for him to leave, but he carried the warmth of this Christmas with him.

When it was time to say goodnight, there was a shared peace between them, an unspoken agreement to take things one day at a time. While the future was unwritten, they had each other—and that was enough.

Our Journey Begins

Day After Christmas

CHRISTMAS HAD COME AND gone, but its warmth lingered in Julie's heart, a reminder of the transformative days she and Robert had shared. They shared memories, opened up about their grief, and, more importantly, had shared their hearts. In those moments, they found their healing together, knitting their lives in ways neither had expected when they met.

Julie smiled, recalling Robert's laughter as they prepared Christmas dinner together. He was packing up his cabin this morning, preparing to head back to the life he had paused for these precious days by the lake. Both of them knew their time here was ending, but there was no sadness—no finality. Instead, there was a promise of more to come, a future they would now face together.

Turning away from the window, Julie sipped her tea, its warmth matching the growing sense of peace in her heart. It felt strange to be so at ease, to feel so hopeful after years spent in the shadow of grief. Ted would have wanted this for her—she knew it. He had always encouraged her to live life to its fullest, and she had learned this, especially since his passing. And now, after five long years, she was ready to embrace life again.

Earlier this morning, Robert helped Julie take down the decorations and put them back in storage. She continued to clean up the cabin as she prepared to leave until she visited again. She looked inside the room where she painted the lake at sunrise she created for Robert. The painting symbolized the fresh start she felt within herself and served as a reminder for Robert of this place and the peace they found together. He took it with him, put it in his car, and packed the rest of his belongings. As she thought of Robert packing his cabin, a mix of gratitude and a twinge of sadness filled her. But she quickly reminded herself of the promise they'd made to each other.

Julie washed and dried the mug she used for her tea. Then she gathered her things, packing with some sense of urgency. Tidying up and packing brought her unexpected comfort. It was her way of preparing herself for what came next. Returning to her life in the city, to her art gallery, and to the world she had left behind for these several days of quiet reflection. But this time, it was different. Something inside her had shifted—she got her life back.

A soft knock at the door interrupted her thoughts. It was Robert.

Opening the door, he had a smile on his face that warmed her heart.

"Ready to go?" he asked.

Julie nodded, returning his smile. "Almost. I just have a few more things to finish."

Robert stepped inside, rubbing his hands together to chase away the cold. "I thought I'd stop by and say goodbye... or rather, see you later."

Julie chuckled at the distinction. "I'm glad you did."

They stood hand in hand, reflecting on their time here. Christmas now felt like a shared journey, not a burden. Julie looked at Robert, feeling a rush of gratitude for everything they had experienced together. She hadn't expected to find someone who understood her so deeply, someone who made the world seem a little brighter.

"I hope the painting reminds you of this place, of us, every time you see it," she said.

"I know it will accomplish that each time, Julie. Thank you again. It means more to me than I can say."

Julie smiled. "I wanted you to remember this place. To remember the peace we found here."

Robert nodded, his eyes misting as he set the painting aside. "I'll cherish it. Just like I'll cherish the time we spent together."

They had found something here that transcended conversation, building a connection through shared pain, healing, and the possibility of new beginnings.

Robert stepped closer, still holding her hands in his. "I don't want this to be the end," he said, pausing. Their eyes met. "I don't want to go back to the way things were. Not without you."

Julie's heart skipped a beat at his words, a mix of relief and hope washing over her. She had been thinking the same thing, but hadn't dared to say it out loud. Now that he had, the path forward felt clear.

"I don't either," she admitted, her voice steady. "I believe this is just the beginning. We'll figure it out—together."

Robert's smile deepened, his hands tightening around hers. "I'd like that. More than anything."

They stood there hand in hand, their futures suddenly brighter than they had seemed in years. The lake, once a place of solitude and healing, had become the backdrop for a new chapter in their lives. A chapter filled with hope, love, and the promise of new beginnings.

Robert spoke, his tone light and teasing. "I look forward to visiting you at your art gallery so we can prepare for our art exhibit."

Julie laughed, his words light and free. "I'll be expecting more sculptures from you. It's time to share your work with the world."

Robert chuckled, nodding in agreement. "I guess it is."

They lingered a little while longer, neither of them quite ready to leave the cabin behind. But when they stepped outside, the crisp air was refreshing and invigorating. The snow crunched beneath their boots as they walked together to their cars. The lake stretched out behind them like a blank canvas, awaiting the next chapter of their lives.

Before parting ways, Robert pulled her into a warm embrace, his arms wrapped tightly around her. Julie closed her eyes, savoring the moment, the warmth of his touch, and the quiet promise of what was to come.

"I'll see you soon," he whispered into her ear.

Julie nodded, her heart full. "Soon, may not be soon enough."

Julie sank into the hug, feeling her life come alive once more. They pulled back, holding hands, and Robert leaned in to kiss Julie on the forehead. Their eyes were tearing up with memories of how this Christmas went, unlike what had been planned, but they were so grateful it happened just the way it did.

And with that, they went their separate ways, but not for long. The road ahead was uncertain, but they were ready to face it together. A new year, a new beginning, and a future filled with hope. As

Julie drove away from the lake. Glancing in the rearview mirror, she watched the cabins fade into the distance. But there was no sadness. She knew she would return to her cabin. This place had become a part of her story, a part of her healing. With Robert by her side, she was ready to face whatever the future held.

Though the lake remained still and frozen, Julie's heart was alive with the promise of a new beginning.

Robert waved as Julie's car disappeared from view, carrying with him a renewed sense of self and the joy of an unforgettable Christmas by the Lake!

The End

Have A Look at my book Christmas on Harmony Lane

If you enjoyed *Christmas by the Lake*, you may also love spending the holidays in a quaint town where Christmas magic has plans.

As snow blankets Harmony Lane and music drifts through frosted windows, the connection grows for Elaine and Tom through shared laughter, small-town traditions, and the comforting rhythm of artistic expression. But opening their hearts again means confronting old fears. Can they open to love after a lifetime of guarding it?

If you're ready for another cozy holiday escape, and you love heartfelt, age-positive Christmas romance filled with warmth, creativity, and new beginnings, you'll adore ***Christmas on Harmony Lane.***

Other Books by Drew Beyson

MOON VIEW SERIES

Love Comes – Prequel

Love Chosen – Book 1 of 3

Love Bonds – Book 2 of 3

Love Lasts – Book 3 of 3

HEARTSTRINGS & DECEPTIONS SERIES

Returning Home – Book 1 of 5

Tangled Webs – Book 2 of 5

Unveiling Truth – Book 3 of 5

Redemption's Promise – Book 4 of 5

Unbreakable Bonds – Book 5 of 5

LOVER'S LIGHTHOUSE SERIES

Light in the Darkness – Book 1 of 6

Whispers of the Past – Book 2 of 6

Tides of Change – Book 3 of 6

Echoes of the Heart – Book 4 of 6

Embracing New Horizons – Book 5 of 6

Harmony by the Sea – Book 6 of 6

CHRISTMAS BY THE LAKE

innercouncilpublications.com

Check out My Moon View Series Prequel - Free Book

Check Out My Moon View Series Prequel — Free Book

As a thank you for reading, I offer a special prequel to the Moon View Series; A warm, heartfelt introduction that captures the moment when everything begins.

To download your free copy, scan the QR code below or go to https://BookHip.com/NABATFJ or visit link below:

InnerCouncilPublications.com

This story is my gift to you. I hope you enjoy your visit to Moon View.

About Author

Drew Beyson writes heartwarming clean romance filled with gentle emotion, hopeful new beginnings, and the quiet magic tucked into everyday life. Her stories invite readers into cozy settings, tender connections, and moments of healing that remind us all that love can bloom in the most unexpected places.

When she isn't writing, Drew enjoys savoring a warm cup of tea or hot chocolate, baking cookies, and taking peaceful strolls in nature. Her time in nature often inspires her stories, characters, and scenes. She treasures the comfort of cozy moments, heartfelt conversations, and the beauty found in slowing down.

To learn more about Drew's books, visit:

innercouncilpublications.com